FOR STACIE, JUSTIN, AND MARK

Aladdin Paperbacks
An imprint of Simon & Schuster
Children's Publishing Division
1230 Avenue of the Americas
New York, NY 10020
First Aladdin Paperbacks edition, 1993
Also available in a hardcover edition from
Simon & Schuster Books for Young Readers
Printed in Hong Kong
10   9   8   7   6   5   4   3
The text of this book is set in ITC Bookman Medium.
The illustrations are rendered in black ink and watercolor.

Library of Congress Cataloging-in-Publication Data
Arnosky, Jim.
Crinkleroot's guide to walking in wild places / by Jim Arnosky.—
1st Aladdin Books ed.
p.   cm.
Originally published: New York: Bradbury Press, 1990.
Summary: Crinkleroot the forest dweller provides tips for walking in
wild places and avoiding such hazards as ticks, poisonous plants,
and wild animals.
ISBN 0-689-71753-9
1. Walking—Juvenile literature.   2. Walking—Safety measures—
Juvenile literature.   3. Wilderness areas—Juvenile literature.
[1. Walking.   2. Safety.   3. Wilderness areas.]   I. Title.
II. Title: Guide to walking in wild places.
[GV199.5.A73   1993]
796.5'1—dc20   92-45775

Crinkleroot's GUIDE TO WALKING IN WILD PLACES

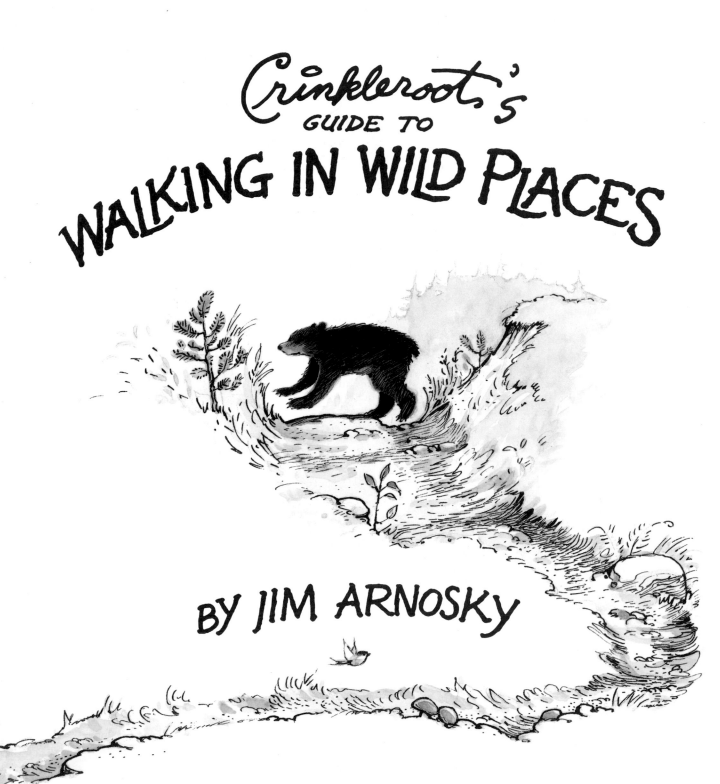

BY JIM ARNOSKY

Aladdin Paperbacks

Hello. My name is Crinkleroot. When I woke up this fine summer morning, my feet were itching to take me places. I'm going for a long walk. You can come, too!

We'll be walking in wild places. You'll need to wear long pants so brush and stickers won't scratch your legs.

In the clearing around my cabin, small birds nest amid the tall grasses and weeds. Look! A song sparrow nestled on her eggs. Let's tiptoe back and away so we won't disturb her.

YOU CAN REMOVE A TICK FROM YOUR CLOTHES BY PUSHING IT OFF USING A TWIG.

ON LONGER HIKES AWAY FROM HOME, I CARRY A TWEEZERS FOR REMOVING ANY TICKS I MAY FIND ON MY SKIN.

What's this? A tick is crawling on my pants! I must have brushed against a grass blade that the tick was on.

When you are walking in weedy or grassy places, stop every so often to check your clothes for ticks. The odds are you won't find any. But if you do happen to find a tick on your clothing, get the tick off before it crawls onto your skin. Ticks bite and suck blood!

5

ABOUT TICKS

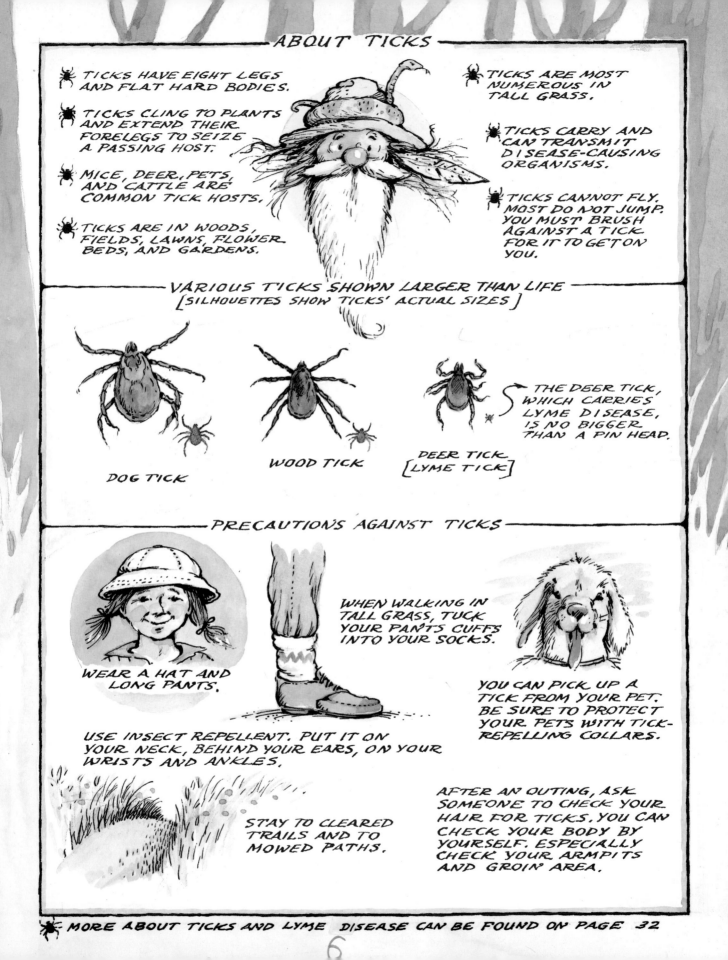

- TICKS HAVE EIGHT LEGS AND FLAT HARD BODIES.
- TICKS CLING TO PLANTS AND EXTEND THEIR FORELEGS TO SEIZE A PASSING HOST.
- MICE, DEER, PETS, AND CATTLE ARE COMMON TICK HOSTS.
- TICKS ARE IN WOODS, FIELDS, LAWNS, FLOWER BEDS, AND GARDENS.

- TICKS ARE MOST NUMEROUS IN TALL GRASS.
- TICKS CARRY AND CAN TRANSMIT DISEASE-CAUSING ORGANISMS.
- TICKS CANNOT FLY. MOST DO NOT JUMP. YOU MUST BRUSH AGAINST A TICK FOR IT TO GET ON YOU.

VARIOUS TICKS SHOWN LARGER THAN LIFE
[SILHOUETTES SHOW TICKS' ACTUAL SIZES]

DOG TICK

WOOD TICK

DEER TICK [LYME TICK]

THE DEER TICK, WHICH CARRIES LYME DISEASE, IS NO BIGGER THAN A PIN HEAD.

PRECAUTIONS AGAINST TICKS

WEAR A HAT AND LONG PANTS.

WHEN WALKING IN TALL GRASS, TUCK YOUR PANTS CUFFS INTO YOUR SOCKS.

YOU CAN PICK UP A TICK FROM YOUR PET. BE SURE TO PROTECT YOUR PETS WITH TICK-REPELLING COLLARS.

USE INSECT REPELLENT. PUT IT ON YOUR NECK, BEHIND YOUR EARS, ON YOUR WRISTS AND ANKLES.

STAY TO CLEARED TRAILS AND TO MOWED PATHS.

AFTER AN OUTING, ASK SOMEONE TO CHECK YOUR HAIR FOR TICKS. YOU CAN CHECK YOUR BODY BY YOURSELF. ESPECIALLY CHECK YOUR ARMPITS AND GROIN AREA.

MORE ABOUT TICKS AND LYME DISEASE CAN BE FOUND ON PAGE 32

Here's a nice clear path beside the brook.

Listen to the running stream. The water
sounds remind me of friendly people chatting,
or children laughing and having fun.

There are fragrant ferns growing along the stream. These ferns smell like freshly mowed hay. They are called hayscented ferns.

WHEREVER YOU WALK, EXCEPT IN DESERT AREAS, YOU ARE LIKELY TO FIND FERNS GROWING ALONG THE TRAILS. HERE ARE FIVE COMMON SPECIES OF FERNS FOR YOU TO LOOK FOR.

CHRISTMAS FERN
36" LONG

SENSITIVE FERN
12" LONG

BRACKEN
36" TALL

MAIDENHAIR
SPLEENWORT
5" LONG

CINNAMON FERN
36" TALL

EBONY
SPLEENWORT
15" LONG

Following a brook, every bend in the stream leads to a fresh new place. Here, where the brook is shaded by trees, the air is cool and damp.

You tread on fallen leaves and pine needles. Thick patches of green moss carpet parts of the trail and cover the tops of stream boulders.

I never wade in water that looks discolored or oily. It could be polluted or littered with broken glass or rusty metal. This brook is so clear and sparkling—I can't resist stepping in!

Wading in a stream, you feel the cool push of moving water. It is the constant motion of the water that wears away the stream stones, making them round and smooth.

In a shallow pool, minnows swim around your legs and nibble at your toes. Hoo! Ha! Hee! That tickles!

14

Walking barefoot is a way to really feel the world, the way the animals do.

Walk flat-footed like a raccoon, and make perfect whole footprints in the wet sand.

Or tiptoe along like a deer, and leave only
toe prints.

When I'm walking barefoot I find all sorts of wonderful things, because I look at the ground carefully before each step. Here's a blue jay feather!

17

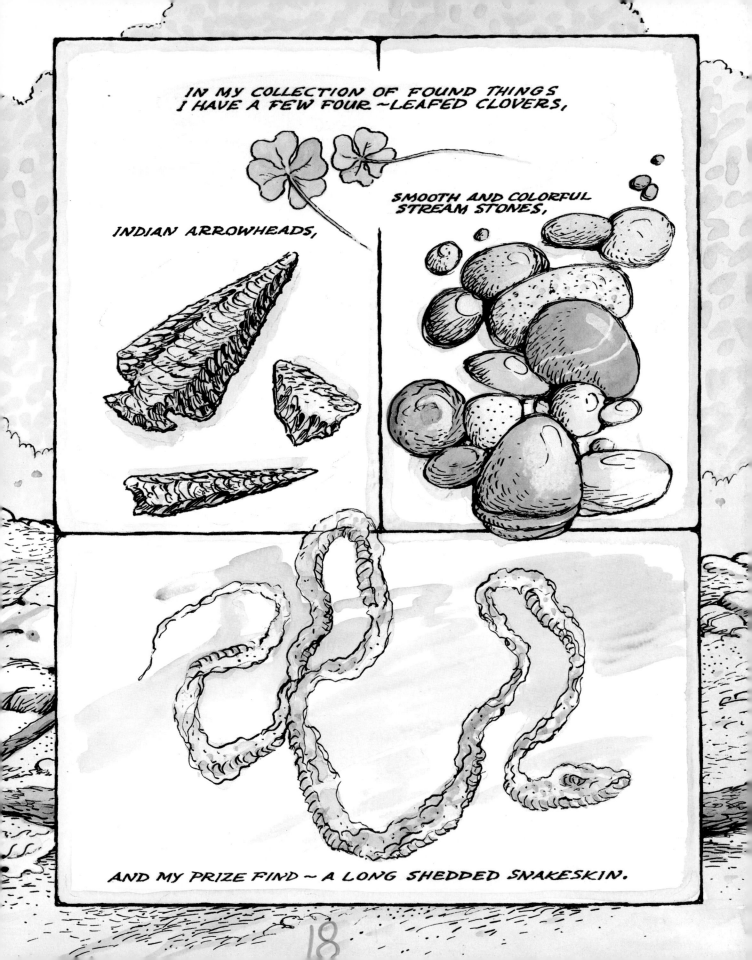

IN MY COLLECTION OF FOUND THINGS
I HAVE A FEW FOUR ~ LEAFED CLOVERS,

SMOOTH AND COLORFUL
STREAM STONES,

INDIAN ARROWHEADS,

AND MY PRIZE FIND ~ A LONG SHEDDED SNAKESKIN.

Before we leave the brook, we had better put our shoes back on.

Hmmm...there's a hornet flying right around me. Maybe it thinks that my yellow shirt is a giant dandelion!

19

HORNET

WASP

HONEYBEE

YELLOW JACKET

IF A HORNET, WASP, OR BEE FLIES CLOSE TO YOU, DON'T RUN OR SWAT THE AIR. YOU MAY PROVOKE A STING.
INSTEAD, REMAIN CALM AND LET THE INSECT FLY AWAY ON ITS OWN.
IF IT SHOULD HAPPEN TO LAND ON YOU, GENTLY BRUSH IT OFF AND WALK AWAY.

IF YOU SEE A HORNET, WASP, OR BEE DISAPPEAR BEHIND THE LEAFY BRANCHES OF A BUSH OR TREE,

OR

FLY INTO AN OPENING IN A HOLLOW LOG,

OR ALIGHT ON THE GROUND AND CRAWL DOWN A HOLE . . . DON'T GO NEAR THAT PLACE!

YOU MAY ACCIDENTALLY BE INVADING A WHOLE NEST OF STINGING HORNETS, OR A HIVE FULL OF ANGRY BEES.

EVEN I AM CAREFUL ABOUT THAT, AND I WAS BORN IN A TREE AND RAISED BY BEES!

NOTE: FOR INFORMATION ABOUT INSECT STINGS, SEE PAGE 32

Rock can be fun to climb and walk over, as long as it isn't too slippery.

Big boulders like this one that are out in the open are kept clean by rains and cleared by wind. They look bare and bald. But in the crevices where windblown dust and other debris collect, soil is created. And in that thin layer of soil, tiny plants and seedling trees grow.

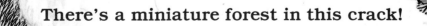

There's a miniature forest in this crack!

At the edge of the woods, plants grow in tangled thickets. You have to search for a gap in the greenery to walk through.

Step back! There's a patch of poison ivy. It grows in sunny places along the borders of woods and streams, on the roadsides, and around old buildings.

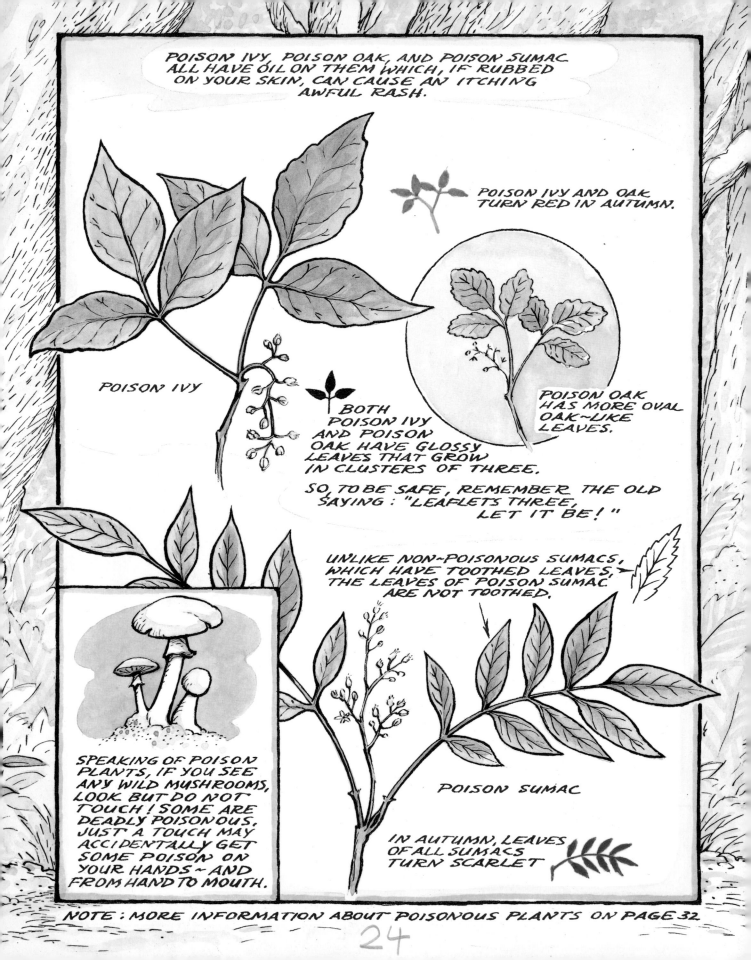

POISON IVY, POISON OAK, AND POISON SUMAC ALL HAVE OIL ON THEM WHICH, IF RUBBED ON YOUR SKIN, CAN CAUSE AN ITCHING AWFUL RASH.

POISON IVY AND OAK TURN RED IN AUTUMN.

POISON IVY

POISON OAK HAS MORE OVAL OAK~LIKE LEAVES.

BOTH POISON IVY AND POISON OAK HAVE GLOSSY LEAVES THAT GROW IN CLUSTERS OF THREE.

SO, TO BE SAFE, REMEMBER THE OLD SAYING: "LEAFLETS THREE, LET IT BE!"

UNLIKE NON~POISONOUS SUMACS, WHICH HAVE TOOTHED LEAVES, THE LEAVES OF POISON SUMAC ARE NOT TOOTHED.

SPEAKING OF POISON PLANTS, IF YOU SEE ANY WILD MUSHROOMS, LOOK BUT DO NOT TOUCH! SOME ARE DEADLY POISONOUS. JUST A TOUCH MAY ACCIDENTALLY GET SOME POISON ON YOUR HANDS ~ AND FROM HAND TO MOUTH.

POISON SUMAC

IN AUTUMN, LEAVES OF ALL SUMACS TURN SCARLET

NOTE: MORE INFORMATION ABOUT POISONOUS PLANTS ON PAGE 32.

The woodland is marked with the footpaths
of animals—tiny footpaths made by mice,
rabbit runs, and deer trails.

All of the trails through the woods have been created simply by the pressing of animals' feet traveling over the same ground day after day.

I've created a footpath of my own. It leads right to the door of my cabin.

After a day outdoors walking in the fields and woods, climbing over rock, and wading in water, my feet deserve a warm bath and a pair of soft slipper socks. Then I like to sit back, put my feet up, and wiggle my toes. How about you?

More tips for walking in wild places

About Ticks

Remove a tick carefully so that the whole tick, head and all, comes off you. Do not squash the tick. It could spread infectious bacteria on you. Rocky Mountain spotted fever is an infection transmitted by a widespread tick found commonly on dogs. Its symptoms are headache, high fever, and severe muscle aches, usually two days after the tick bite. A characteristic spotty rash begins on the soles of the feet and palms of the hands and spreads. Lyme disease has fewer immediate symptoms. If you develop a mysterious stainlike rash, see your doctor. It could be an early sign of Lyme disease. Tell your doctor about every tick bite and ask about treatment that may be necessary to protect you from disease. Once detected, both Rocky Mountain spotted fever and Lyme disease can be successfully treated.

About Insect Stings

Wasps, hornets, and bumblebees can sting repeatedly. Only honeybees lose their stingers when they sting. Remove a stinger by scraping it out with your fingernail or some other flat-edged object. Do not use tweezers. You may squeeze the stinger's venom sac and push more venom into your skin. After being stung, if you show signs of severe allergic reaction—swelling badly or a rash, especially on other parts of your body away from the sting, such as your eyes, mouth, etc., see a doctor immediately. If you are not terribly allergic to being stung, you can treat a sting yourself by washing the area with soap and water and applying an ice pack to the spot to reduce any minor swelling that may occur.

About Poisonous Plants

After accidentally touching a poisonous plant, don't rub or scratch your skin. Go home and take off any clothing that may have also touched the plant. The plant's invisible oil will be on the fabric. Then gently wash the oil off your skin with warm soapy water, and pat yourself dry.

About Wild Animals

Most snakes are nonpoisonous and harmless. They will scoot away as soon as they sense your approaching footsteps. If you see a snake and you are not sure if it is poisonous, give it plenty of room. A snake can strike out a distance a little over one-third of the length of its body.

Never corner a wild animal. If it cannot flee, it will fight. Never pet a wild animal, even if it seems unafraid of you. You may accidentally provoke a bite, or the animal may be sick and dangerous.

Finally, don't let the few hazards that exist outdoors keep you from enjoying the countless pleasures that can be experienced in the woods, fields, and waters.

Your friend,

Crinkleroot